For Joanne and Judy,
good, old friends.
—HZ

For my brother.
—RD

Text copyright © 2001 by Harriet Ziefert
Illustrations copyright © 2001 by Rebecca Doughty
G. P. PUTNAM'S SONS,
a division of Penguin Putnam Books for Young Readers,
345 Hudson Street, New York, NY 10014.
G. P. Putnam's Sons, Reg. U.S. Pat. & Tm. Off. Published simultaneously in Canada.
Printed in China for Harriet Ziefert, Inc. Jacket designed by Gina DiMassi.
The art was done in Flashe paint and ink on Bristol board.
Library of Congress Cataloging-in-Publication Data
Ziefert, Harriet. 39 uses for a friend / Harriet Ziefert;
illustrated by Rebecca Doughty. p. cm. Brief text and illustrations describe
how a friend can be an alarm clock, back scratcher, comedian, worm handler,
listener, and more. [1. Friendship—Fiction.] I. Title: Thirty-nine uses for a friend.
II. Doughty, Rebecca, 1955- ill. III. Title. PZ7.Z487 Aac 2001 [E]—dc21 00-068414
ISBN 0-399-23616-3
1 3 5 7 9 10 8 6 4 2
First Impression

39 Uses
for a Friend

Harriet Ziefert
drawings by **Rebecca Doughty**

G. P. Putnam's Sons   New York

trailblazer

accomplice

guard

hairdresser

sprinkler

storyteller

model

manicurist

coach

chef

listener

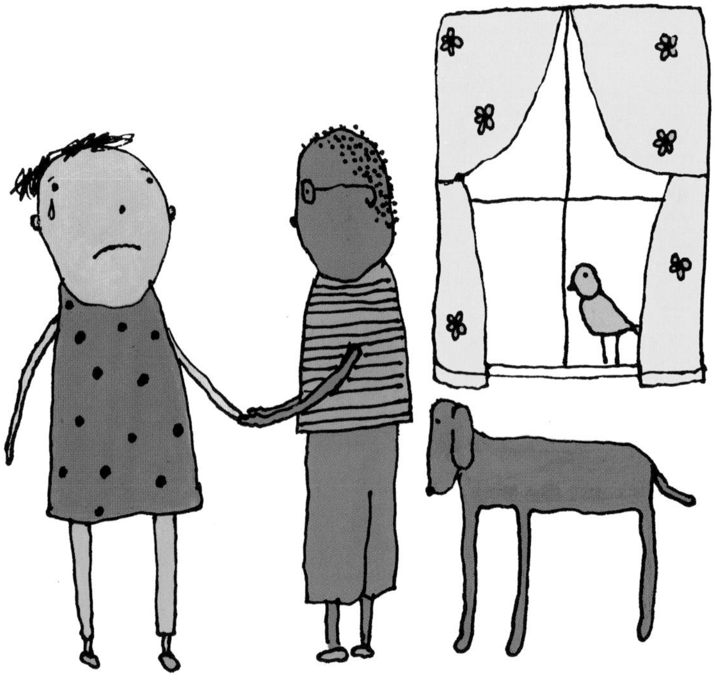

backrest

dancing partner

air conditioner

perfume sniffer

hand holder

comedian

copilot

pillow

ladder

taxi

timekeeper

photographer

doctor

bug remover

lamp holder

best friends today...

...and tomorrow.